MW00975643

The Bumblebee Cousins

Wyatt and Nolan Search for the Truth

The Bumblebee Cousins

Cousins

Wyatt and Nolan Search
for the Truth

by *Deb Thomalla*

Blessings!
Deb Thomalla

tate publishing
CHILDREN'S DIVISION

Published by Tate Publishing & Enterprises, LLC
127 E. Trade Center Terrace | Mustang, Oklahoma 73064 USA
1.888.361.9473 | www.tatepublishing.com

Tate Publishing is committed to excellence in the publishing industry. The company reflects the philosophy established by the founders, based on Psalm 68:11,
"The Lord gave the word and great was the company of those who published it."

Book design copyright © 2011 by Tate Publishing, LLC. All rights reserved.
Cover and interior design by Stan Perl
Illustrations by Justin Stier

Published in the United States of America

ISBN: 978-1-61346-732-9
1. Juvenile Fiction / Animals / General
2. Juvenile Fiction / Family / General
11.12.01

For my grandchildren,
Live with the knowledge
and assurance that God's
Grace is all you need to "fly."

Acknowledgments

To Jesus Christ, for the gifts of writing and courage, for divine inspiration and timing, and for His grace that is always sufficient.

For my life's journey that gave me the insight for this book and for the insight the book gave me for my life's journey.

For my husband, Tom, and our children and their spouses, Erin and Dale, Angie and Brent, Katie and Joe, and Tommy and Brianna, for believing I could "fly" when I didn't think I could.

For the entire Gerald and Donna Thomalla family who were the inspiration for most of my characters.

For my grandchildren and their unconditional love, the most amazing gifts God has ever given me.

We are all nurtured by as many people as there are petals on a peony. For my peony petals, for all your love and support.

For Tate Publishing, providing me with this amazing opportunity.

For my parents, Chuck and Gert Zerfas, who made it possible in so many ways for me to accept this opportunity to invest in my dream.

Table of Contents

The Granite Garden

Spring had finally arrived in central Minnesota after a long, cold winter. The daisies, daffodils, tulips, and lilacs were opening their faces to the warmth of the sun. The blossoms of the fruit trees filled the air with the sweet fragrances of their nectar. The granite garden was renewed by the spring rains and coming to life with the buzzing, hovering, and fluttering of everyone returning from their winter migrations. It was the first spring migration for Wyatt and the second for Nolan, the Bumblebee Cousins.

Wyatt and Nolan had been best buds since Wyatt hatched in that very garden. They were proud to be great-grandsons of Queen Bee Donna Mae. Being the queen meant she was the wisest bee in the garden. Everyone in the garden went to her for answers to any problems or questions. Queen Bee Donna Mae had roving reporter drones, male worker bees buzzing about the garden. They reported everything to her. If the bumblebees got into any mischief or trouble, she knew about it. Queen Bee Donna Mae was one tough granny.

As they sunned themselves on the great granite rock in the center of the garden, Nolan savored his daffodil nectar and daisy dewdrops. Wyatt had inhaled his snack and hovered over Nolan, impatiently waiting for him to finish.

"Hurry up, Nolan. Do you have to be such a pokey eater? I need to know who everyone else is that lives in the garden."

When he finally finished, Nolan hovered above Wyatt like a helicopter spinning in circles, counting. "One, two, three, four, five—that's how many times I've told you who everyone is! Why can't you remember, Wyatt?"

"I'm sorry, Nolan, but you know how nervous and excited I get, and when I get nervous and excited, I can't remember a thing. I'm so excited to meet all of our neighbors, and I'm afraid I won't remember their names." explained Wyatt, pleadingly.

"Oh, all right," Nolan conceded, "but this is it. I'm not telling you again!"

"Thank you, thank you, Nolan! I won't ask you again," Wyatt promised, as he started to hug his cousin.

"No hugging in front of everyone! Now sit still and pay attention. And stop getting so nervous already!"

Getting to Know the Neighbors

"Well," Nolan began, "you know our best buddies, Johnny, J-Rod, Andrew, and Gage, the fearless Dragonfly Boys."

"Yes, I know, I know, but I don't see them anywhere!" worried Wyatt.

"Remember, they volunteered for our garden safety patrol? They are out on their morning drills."

"Oh, yes. Isn't that scary General Jessica Damselfly their leader?"

"Yes, sir!" Nolan saluted. "And she has no mercy for those boys whatsoever! Over there"—Nolan pointed—"on the tallest sunflower are the ladybugs, Michelle, Stacy, Dora, Marie, and Katherine. You can remember them because they're always taking a head count of all of us kids in the garden. They watch over us like they're our mothers or something."

"Or they count each other's age spots, right?" Wyatt giggled.

"Yep, good job, little buddy! Now just above the ladybugs are the fireflies, Mikey, Justin, and Jay, napping in the apple blossoms."

"Where?" asked Wyatt. "I don't see them."

"Of course you can't see them right now," Nolan said, rolling his eyes. "They only light up at night!"

"Then how do you know they are up there, smarty?"

"Because I can see the apple blossom petals flopping back and forth every time they snore. See?" Wyatt and Nolan giggled as they watched the petals moving back and forth, back and forth, back and forth.

Next, Nolan pointed to the Butterfly Beauties, Sophia, Diana, and Kara, sunning themselves while floating on lily pads in the pond. "And annoyingly buzzing around above them are Adam, Steven, and T.C., members of the Horsefly Gang."

"I'm supposed to steer clear of them, right?" asked Wyatt.

"That's for sure, unless you want to spend the summer stuck in Camp Web!" stressed Nolan.

"See, fluttering over the pond, those are the Mayfly Girls, Bethany, Jenny, Emma, and Keeley, admiring their new wing-bling."

Nolan and Wyatt looked at each other and, pretending to be sick, in unison said, "Girls, yuck!"

"See that June bug and flying ant in the clearing?" Wyatt asked. "What are they doing?"

"Oh, that's Jack June Bug getting flying lessons from Phil Flying Ant," said Nolan, shaking his head.

"Huh, flying lessons?" questioned Wyatt.

"You will see for yourself soon enough, little cuz. Do you remember those five guys leaning on the back fence sipping barley brew and getting the latest buzz?" Nolan asked.

"Are they David, Alan, Tyler, Jesse, and JP, the Worker Bees?" replied Wyatt, with a hopeful grin.

"Right!" exclaimed Nolan, as he gave Wyatt a high-five wing tap. "They are also the queen's roving reporters."

With his chest puffed out with pride, Wyatt said, "And I know who lives in the hive, tucked snuggly beneath the royal red rose bushes—Queen Bee Donna Mae and Sir Gerald, her loyal silent servant.

"Shhh!" Nolan scolded, "You do not want the queen to hear you call him her silent servant! We all know he is, but if any of her roving reporters hear you call him anything besides 'Sir Gerald,' well, you're too young to know what will happen!"

"Okay," whispered Wyatt, "is that everyone? I'm getting dizzy trying to remember," he asked, while buzzing around in circles.

"Yes, that is everyone who lives in the garden, but that's not why you're getting dizzy. Now let's get busy pollinating."

Believing the Unbelievable

As the Bumblebee Cousins busied themselves with pollinating the lilacs, the peace-
ful garden was beginning to hum, whir, and
buzz with the excitement of news. And news
travels fast in small gardens. The sounds grew
louder and louder. Wyatt noticed the noise
first. Looking around to see what was hap-
pening, he saw that everyone was heading
for the great, granite rock in the center of the
garden. He got Nolan's attention, and they
buzzed over to the rock too.

The Ladybugs were frantically trying to keep track of everyone; the Horse-fly Gang buzzed right into the middle of the excitement as the Fearless Dragonflies, led by General Jessica, patrolled the garden perimeters, keeping watch for predators.

Phil Flying Ant quickly crawled on top of Jack June Bug's back, hoping to help him navigate to the gathering without running into something. But with his fear of flying, Jack scrunched his eyes shut as he took to the air. Phil yelled, "Right, Jack! More to the right!" Smack. Jack flew right into the side of the granite rock, bounced off, and landed flat on his back, spinning in circles on the ground. Phil burrowed his way out from under him gasping for air. Shaking his head he said, "Your other right, Jack."

Wyatt asked Nolan, "Flying lessons?"

"Uh-huh," replied Nolan, as they burst into laughter.

There was so much racket that the Fireflies even flickered to life. The Mayfly Girls giggled, and the Butterfly Beauties fluttered in, fashionably late. The Worker Bees worked the crowd for tidbits of information that they could report to the queen for some of her barley brew nectar. The crowd was gathered on the granite rock.

Suddenly from high above them, like bombers at the speed of sound, the Hornet Twins grazed the crowd. With all eyes on them, they circled and landed in the middle of the now silent gathering. While Nolan had been reviewing the names of everyone in the garden with Wyatt, the twins, Lilly and Lila, had been buzzing the garden, and baiting everyone to the great granite rock with juicy tidbits of information.

Lilly arrogantly hovered and nodded acknowledgement to the crowd. "Ladies and gentlemen, boys and girls of this ever-so-small and insignificant garden, Lila and I bring you the latest aerodynamic discovery."

The crowd responded with gasps, oohs, and ahs.

"You see, privileged as we are, Lila and I spent our migration at the renowned Kennedy Space Center while the rest of you frolicked aimlessly at Disney World. What we are about to tell you is, in fact, so news-worthy that you will want to be certain to inform Queen Bee Donna Mae, even though she does not deserve her title."

The crowd buzzed with excited anticipation of news worthy of their queen's attention.

"As you can see," Lilly added, "my beautiful, identical twin has summoned the homely, worthless Bumblebee Cousins to center stage. The discovery we are about to reveal is specific to bumblebees. An aerodynamicist at the German Institute of Physics has calculated a mathematical theory. The theory calculates that the dimensions of bumblebees' wings relative to their body mass leaves them utterly and pitifully incapable of flying."

The audience response was puzzled looks and quizzical murmuring—nothing near the dramatic turmoil Lilly had intended to create.

Lila shoved her stunned sister out of the way and shouted, "What she means is that scientists have discovered that bumblebee wings are too pathetically small to lift their disgustingly fat bodies!"

The crowd roared with simultaneous reactions.

"What?"

"Why?"

"I don't believe you!"

"Just try and prove it; we know you are wrong!"

Then Nolan shouted, "Stop! Quiet, please!"

"Sh-Sh-Sh-Shush!" Wyatt added. He was so nervous he stammered and his cheeks blushed cherry red. The crowd grew quiet.

Nolan confidently stated, "That is simply nonsense. Everyone knows that bumblebees fly from the first moment of life until our last dying breath." The crowd nodded in agreement.

Nolan flapped his wings for takeoff. Nothing happened. He flapped harder. Still nothing happened. Wyatt flapped his wings as hard as he could. Nothing! The cousins flapped and flapped and took running leaps until their tiny legs gave out beneath them and their wings hung limply at their sides. The Horse-fly Gang roared with laughter as they buzzed away. The Butterfly Beauties blushed with embarrassment for them, and the Worker Bees raced to the queen's hive. The rest of the crowd slowly dispersed, whispering and shaking their heads.

Nolan laid there on the cold slab of granite in disbelief. Tears rolled down his cheeks. He was speechless and paralyzed with fear.

Wyatt was so afraid he stood there trembling and stammering, "Who-who-who are they? Wh-wh-why did they do that? H-h-how could they . . . ? Wha-wha-what are we going to do?" Nolan just stared into space. Wyatt yelled to get his attention. "Nolan! Who are those two hornets? Why and how did they make us lose our ability to fly? And what are we going to do to fix our wings?"

"They are the hornet twins, Lilly and Lila. I don't know why they did that. I don't know how they did that. I don't know what we are going to do," Nolan responded in monotone.

General Jessica Damselfly and the Dragonfly Guards came to their rescue. They loaded the bumblebees on cots and carried them to the hive of Queen Bee Donna Mae.

Her wisdom would be needed to solve their dilemma.

Lilly and Lila had slipped away amidst the chaos. Their mission was accomplished.

The Family Feud

Long before the Bumblebee Cousins or the Hornet Twins were even twinkles in their daddies' eyes, a family feud had taken place. You see, Lilly and Lila's great-grandmother, Rosie Rae, is Queen Bee Donna Mae's older cousin.

It was tradition in the bumblebee queendom that the oldest granddaughter of the reigning queen would inherit the throne. However, Rosie Rae had eloped with her aeronautic-school sweetheart, leaving her arranged mate behind. The punishment for her disobedience to the queen was losing her bumblebee status. Rosie Rae became a family outcast. She and her descendants were permanently demoted to hornets. Her grandmother passed the family crown to Donna Mae instead.

Rosie Rae and her family continued a bitter hatred and jealousy of the queen bee and her descendants. What Lilly and Lila did to Wyatt and Nolan was simply another attack on the royal family. The boys, however, were not yet aware of the family history.

Humility

Wyatt was determined to get his questions answered. He knocked on the great door of the hive. The queen's servant, Sir Gerald, opened the door and stood looking at the Bumblebee Cousins. Nolan nudged Wyatt and whispered, "Say something; don't just stand there staring!"

Shaking violently on his tiny legs, Wyatt shouted, "We-we-we-we need to see the Queen B-B-B-Bee."

Sir Gerald said, "Humph," and slammed the door in their faces.

"Now what?" exclaimed Nolan, as tears began to stream down his frightened little face again.

But just as quickly as he'd left, Sir Gerald was back. "Queen says to bring her some sweet barley brew, then she'll see you." Sir Gerald stated in monotone. Then he slammed the door again.

"But, but, wait!" shouted Wyatt, "How are we supposed to get to the barley fields when we can't fly?"

Nolan shrugged and said, "I guess we walk."

Sweat and Perseverance

Now walking is no easy task for bumble-bees. The farthest the boys had ever walked was around the center of a flower. But they knew they must see the queen if they were ever to fly again, so they set out on the long difficult journey ahead.

It was dark and damp on the ground. They were surrounded by a thick maze of towering blades of grass, daisies that seemed to touch the clouds, and trees so big it would take a week for them to walk around one.

"Which way do we go?" asked Wyatt

"I know the barley field is outside the garden behind the queen's roses. So first we need to make our way over this gigantic sand hill," replied Nolan, with a sigh.

They began trudging up the hill when an ant carrying five times his own weight stopped and asked, "What are you bumblebees doing down here with us ants?"

"We can't fly, and we need to get some barley nectar for Queen Bee Donna Mae so she'll tell us how to fly again," Nolan explained.

The ant put down his load, whistled, and yelled, "Hey, Joe, come and help me. These boys need a lift. This is my brother, Smokin' Joe, and my name is Dumper Dan."

The boys squealed with excitement as they climbed onto the ants' backs.

"Now don't go getting too excited," Dan said. "We're carpenter ants, and we work from sunup to sundown, so we can only take you to the other side of this construction site."

Wyatt and Nolan rested their legs and watched in amazement as the other ants worked with speed and precision. When they got over the hill, the ants set them down. Dan pointed out a pine tree in the distance. "Keep heading for that tree so you don't get lost."

Joe added, "It's going to take a lot of sweat and perseverance for you two to get to that barley field."

"I'm pretty sure all the walking will have us sweating plenty," said Nolan.

"Yes, but where do we get that per-se-ver-ance stuff?" Wyatt asked.

Joe and Dan looked at each other and walked away, shaking their heads.

The Bumblebee Cousins were on their own again. Feeling rested and optimistic, they headed for the pine tree. They marched and sang, "The ants go marching one by one hur-rah, hurrah . . ." to distract themselves from the daunting distance ahead.

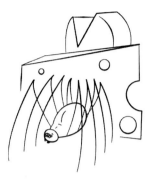

Spiders to the Rescue

Suddenly a tiny black, eight-legged creature scurried around them, stopping them in their tracks. "And just where do you think you're going?" she snapped. Nolan plopped down on his bottom. Wyatt began to tell their story but was abruptly interrupted.

"I am Mardelle Wonder-Spider, and I am not interested in your story so just get to the point," she said, while tapping her four left feet impatiently. "I can take care of everything for everybody. I'm a small wonder, and I can solve bigger problems better than anyone else you'll ever meet. I'm busy, so just tell me what you need."

Wyatt began, "We have to get to the barley field to—"

"Spare me the details, sonny. Tuck your wings, curl up your legs, and roll along on the web I'll spin behind me. I'll get you as far as that pine tree up ahead." So roll they did, giggling all the way.

"Wee! This is fun," exclaimed Nolan.

Mardelle Wonder-Spider spun a web all the way to the pine tree in record time. In fact, she was so fast the only one who had ever caught her in his web was Rollie Daddy Longlegs. Without so much as a warning, Mardelle abruptly stopped spinning her web and dropped the boys at the feet of the longest legs they had ever laid eyes on. As she sped out of sight, she yelled, "Rollie Daddy, take care of these two. I've got work to do."

"I'd be delighted," responded Rollie. "You lads appear to be quite weary; may I offer you something to eat?" But before the bumbles could respond, Rollie went on, "How about some cheese? I have sharp cheddar, swiss, and a spicy pepper jack. No, no, I believe a smooth mild marble jack would be a more favorable choice for you lads, but I only have one serving left . . ."

Waiting politely for an opportunity to tell Rollie that they appreciated his offer, Nolan and Wyatt fell fast asleep while this sophisticated, debonair gentleman finished his litany of cheeses. When they awoke two hours later, Rollie was still reciting his list of cheeses, giving a precise description of each. Nolan cleared his throat to get Rollie's attention.

"Oh, my, please forgive my ramblings. I do love the topic of cheese."

"No need for an apology, but we do need to get to the barley field. Could you please point us in the right direction?" Wyatt asked.

"Nonsense. I'll not have you walking all that way. Climb up on top of my legs. You can ride. I've got eight legs, and mine were made for walking."

The boys gladly accepted the ride. They lay on the crook between Rollie's body and his knees. Propping their wings under their heads, they gazed up at the starry sky until the swaying motion lulled them back to sleep.

Dawn was just a sliver on the horizon when Rollie stopped at the edge of a pond.

"I'm sorry, lads, but swimming I cannot do. I must turn back. I do wish you the best in your travels."

"Thank you so much, Rollie Daddy. You've already gone above and beyond in your helpfulness," stated Nolan.

"Ditto that," Wyatt added.

The Water Way

The cousins stared out over the lime-green slime-covered water. Nolan burst into tears, overwhelmed with despair. Wyatt put a wing around his cousin, trying to make him feel better.

"What's all this blubbering about? You are going to raise the water level if you don't stop crying."

Looking around to find where the voice came from, Nolan whimpered, "We don't know how to get to the other side of the pond."

"We can't fly right now and we don't know how to swim." explained Wyatt.

"Now, now, you two, calm down. I'll help you."

"Where are you? And who are you?" Nolan asked, while wiping away his tears with the back of his wings.

"I'm out here, on the water. My name is Merry Mary Water Beetle. Why are you little bumblebees sitting on the ground? Why can't you fly to the other side of the pond?" Wyatt and Nolan told Merry Mary what had happened and where they were headed. She listened intently and patiently as they described every detail of their journey. When they'd finished, Mary said, "If you'll wait here, I'll gather my family. I believe we can help you cross the pond."

"Really? That would save us the three days it would take to walk around to the other side!" exclaimed Nolan.

"Yes, really," Merry Mary assured them, as she squiggled away atop the water. She and a dozen fellow water beetles returned with a petal from a water lily in tow. "You boys climb into the petal and relax. We'll ferry you to the other side before you know it."

The boys lay as still as they could, eyes wide with fear. They had never floated on water and certainly didn't know how to swim. Sooner than they expected, they were on the opposite shore. They jumped to dry land and waved good-bye. Nolan and Wyatt stood watching the beetles zigzag away, their wakes forming an amazing pattern through the green slime that coated the top of the pond.

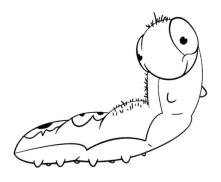

A Warm and Fuzzy Day

Wyatt and Nolan trudged along. The high afternoon sun had them sweating profusely. Nolan commented, "I think we got the sweating figured out."

"Now if we could only find some of that per-se-ver-ance, we'd know for sure that we were getting close to the barley field," Wyatt added.

Growing weary with hunger, they stopped on the crest of a hill to rest. Before setting out again, they looked ahead for a landmark to go toward. Nolan said, "I think I must be delirious from the sun or hunger or both. I think I see a garden up ahead."

"Then we're both delirious, because I see it too!" exclaimed Wyatt, as he ran as fast as his little legs could carry him. They ran right to the sweet peas. With their eyes closed in sheer delight, they buried their faces in the blossoms. They drank the delicious nectar, unaware that the gardener was watching them.

Warm, fuzzy Arlene Caterpillar smiled lovingly as they filled their hungry tummies. Nolan stopped to savor the sweetness and opened his eyes to the surprise of Arlene. Speechless, he nudged Wyatt, who continued to guzzle and gulp the nectar. Nolan poked Wyatt in the side with the point of his wing to get his attention.

"What?" asked Wyatt, annoyed by the interruption. When Nolan didn't answer, Wyatt looked up and, seeing Arlene, said, "Oh . . . hi . . . you have a really nice garden."

"Thank you," Arlene said, grinning at their surprise. "It's okay. Keep eating. I certainly don't grow all of this to look at."

"Oh, thank you, ma'am. We're sorry we didn't ask first," said Nolan, relieved by Arlene's friendly response.

"Yes, thanks," Wyatt said, as he buried his head in another blossom. Once they had their fill and introductions were exchanged, the boys told Arlene Caterpillar their dilemma.

She said, "Come with me. I can show you the barley field." The bumble boys were speechless. Arlene inched along gracefully, the rise and fall of her body smooth and rhythmic as a waltz. Thinking her movement looked effortless, Wyatt attempted to maneuver like a caterpillar. Standing on his tiptoes, holding his wings in a dance-like pose, he rolled forward onto his tummy. Splat. He planted his face firmly into the rich, black dirt of the garden. At the far end of the garden, just beyond the sweet corn, lay an ocean of golden grain.

"There it is," said Arlene. "There's the barley field."

The bumbles' mouths gaped in awe. "We don't mean to be rude, Miss Caterpillar . . ." began Wyatt.

"I understand," Arlene said warmly, as she gave the Bumblebee Cousins each a warm, fuzzy hug and sent them on their way.

Going for the Gold

Giddy with relief, the cousins rolled down the gradual slope landing at the foot of the stocks of barley. Looking up, up, up the stocks to the distant heads of grain, their laughter stopped instantly. It was the last straw. They had come all this way only to find the impossible. There was no way for the little bumbles to harvest the barley nectar.

Nolan began sobbing hysterically. Wyatt laid there covering his head with his wings. They didn't see the stalk of barley about to topple right on top of them. Suddenly, they heard, "Timber!" just in time to roll out of the way. There between them, only an antenna's width away, laid a big ripe head of barley with a locust on top.

"Gee whiz, lady. You could have killed us!" shouted Wyatt.

"Oh my golly gee willakers, I'm so sorry! I was daydreaming, and the next thing I knew . . . well, here we are, all cozy. What are you two little bumbles doing on the ground in the first place?"

"No, no ma'am, it's our fault. We shouldn't have been in your way," said Nolan, giving Wyatt a wide-eyed look as if to say, be quiet. "We won't take up your time with our story, ma'am. We'll just get what we came for and be on our way," Nolan offered politely.

"Nonsense, I love a great story. Come, we'll sit around my campfire, and you can tell it to me. That will give me a chance to sample the latest batch of Queenie's barley brew before it ships out tomorrow. Would you boys like to sample the special nectar used to make her highness's brew? And you can call me Gin or Roman, no more of this formal ma'am stuff," she said.

In unison the boys replied, "Yes, ma'am."

As she stoked the campfire, she explained, "My full name is Lady Ginger Locust, so Gin for short. But, since I roam off a lot, my friends nicknamed me Roman."

"He's Nolan, and I'm Wyatt. We're cousins. We're Queenie's great-grandsons, and she sent us here to get her some barley brew before she will tell us how to fly again," blurted Wyatt.

"I'm lost already. Why don't you have a seat and start at the beginning of your story, okay?" Ginger offered. Lady Locust gave the boys some barley nectar and drank her barley brew, as the Bumblebee Cousins began recounting the adventures of the past two days.

A Case for Granny

"Wow, you boys should write a book," Ginger said, as she polished off her third bottle of barley brew.

"Roman!" yelled a deep, gruff voice, startling Wyatt and Nolan. "Have you been sitting here sipping barley brews all night?"

"Oh, Al, relax. What's the problem?" she replied calmly. "Boys, don't let his loud voice scare you. He just uses volume to make up for what he lacks in size. Meet my boss, Inchworm Al. Al, these are Queen Bee Donna Mae's great-grandsons, Wyatt and Nolan."

"I can see the family resemblance. So what did she send you two out here for? No, wait, let me guess. Some hornets told you that you couldn't fly. So you went to Queenie for help, but she said you have to get her some barley brew first. Then she'll help you," Al said, with a wink.

"Yes, but how . . . ?" Nolan began.

"You aren't the first two bumblebees she's pulled this—I mean, sent out here. I remember a few years back she sent Tom and Deb Bumblebee. It was raining and the grain was soggy . . ."

"Tom and Deb Bumblebee? They're our grandpa and grandma!" said Wyatt excitedly.

"Follow me, boys. I have just what you need. Plus I'll have you home before sunset tonight." The boys followed him thinking it was cool that they could walk as fast as Inchworm Al could inch.

Al explained everything to the boys. "I'm the master brewer of Sweet Barley Gold, the queen's special recipe. When a new batch is ready, it's bottled and packaged a dozen bottles to a case. Next, my shed crew loads the case onto Goldie Goldfinch's back. She makes the delivery right to the queen's door, and Queenie's old, gold-toothed silent servant, Sir Gerald, hauls it all in the hive and serves it to her. And as if that weren't enough, she only lets him have one bottle from each batch. That's what she thinks, anyway."

"Inchworm Al, that's an amazing process. But how does it help us get back home?" asked Nolan.

"Come with me," he replied. Al had his shed crew pack only eleven bottles in the next case. "Now there's room for the two of you."

"Wow! You mean we get to ride in the case on Goldie Goldfinch's back, and she'll take us right to the queen?" exclaimed Wyatt.

"You've got it, sonny. Now in you two go," Al said.

Wyatt and Nolan grinned and giggled with joy. It had been two nights and three days since they left home, and they would be back in less than an hour.

Where the Truth Lies

Sir Gerald removed the lid of the case. He grinned so big when he saw the boys inside that the sun's reflection off his gold-capped teeth nearly blinded them. Sir Gerald giggled so hard he was practically dancing a jig. He helped the boys out of the case and carried it in to the queen, motioning for Wyatt and Nolan to follow him.

Trembling with excitement, the boys bowed before Queen Bee Donna Mae. They didn't dare get back up until she gave the command. Sir Gerald served her a goblet of the Sweet Barley Gold. She took her time sipping her special nectar recipe. It felt like an hour before she finally spoke.

"I'm impressed. You may rise. You accomplished your mission in just three days and two nights. You beat the current record, set by your own grandparents, Tom and Deb Bumblebee. So I take it you met Joe and Dan Carpenter Ants, Wonder-Spider, Mardelle, Merry Mary, Inchworm Al, and the others?" Queen Bee asked. The boys stood there shocked, jaws dropped, mouths open, and speechless.

"My roving reporters," she explained, then she took another sip. "You'd better sit down for what I'm about to tell you. Nolan, Wyatt, the truth is, you can fly. In fact, you always could."

"B-b-b-but—" began Wyatt.

"Hush now," she commanded, "let me finish. Come up here, boys. Come and sit on Great Granny's lap. The only reason you couldn't fly was because you chose to believe what others said about you. What you believe about yourself is powerful. Whether true or false, what you believe determines how you live your life. When you chose to believe Lilly and Lila's misinformation about bumblebees being too fat for their wings to carry them, your lives became much more difficult, right?" The boys nodded in agreement. "Is there anything you would like to say to Lilly and Lila?" asked Queen Bee.

"Yes, ma'am!" Wyatt began, "I would tell them that it is wrong to lie and even worse to embarrass us in front of everyone in our garden."

"It's especially bad to bully others because they are a different shape, size, or color than you are," Nolan added.

Next she asked, "Wyatt and Nolan, what do you think would be an appropriate punishment for Lilly and Lila?"

"I think they should apologize to us and everyone in the garden," Nolan said.

"Yes!" Wyatt agreed, "And they should have to walk everywhere for a whole day with nobody helping them."

"I agree with both of your recommendations. I will explain this to Lilly and Lila as well as their parents. I want the two of you to supervise them on the day they spend walking," stated Queen Bee.

"Thank you, Great Grandmother!" they exclaimed. Then they both kissed her on her cheeks.

"Wyatt and Nolan," their great grandmother instructed, "I want you to always remember that God created each of us to be just as we are with a special purpose in mind. Don't let anyone convince you of anything different. Believe in yourselves. Life won't always be easy, but you will fly every 'step' of the way.

"I'll let the two of you decide if you will share this lesson with your younger siblings and cousins, or let them learn it on their own." Queen Bee Donna Mae winked as she took another sip from her goblet. Wyatt and Nolan looked at each other and grinned mischievously.

Epilogue

Is it aerodynamically impossible for a bumblebee's wings to carry its own weight?

According to Cecil Adams, in the 1930s an aerodynamics expert was asked that very question.

"According to theory of the day, bumblebees didn't generate enough lift to fly" (Adams).

The next day, the aerodynamicist recalculated and found that he had been mistaken, but he was too late to correct himself publicly. The story spread far and wide and became embedded in folklore.

The original calculations were based on the analogy between airplanes and bees. However, bumblebees fly on the same principal as a helicopter, not an airplane, giving them the ability to lift, hover, spin, and fly forward.

Bibliography

Adams, Cecil. "Is it Aerodynamically Impossible for Bumblebees to Fly?" A Straight Dope Classic from Cecil's Storehouse of Human Knowledge. http://www.straight-dope.com/ (accessed August 25, 2010).